Listen to Me!

Glurk!

Islington

BOOK**S**WAP

Please take me home!
(better still, swap me with one of yours!)

Funny stories, sad stories, mystery stories, scary stories, stories about school, stories about friends, stories about animals, stories about family. If you liked this story book, we've got lots more like it that you can borrow from our libraries!

Join your local Islington Library today!
www.islington.gov.uk/libraries

3 0120 02576964 8

"Listen, everybody!"
sang Pru.

"I am going to amaze you
with my pretty Pru Prance...
Everybody?"

Where was everybody?

Tilly and the others were all inside.
They were singing and dancing with Hector.

"There's nothing more
I like to do than to dance
the Wiggle-Wiggle Woo!"

"I like to shake,
I like to bop…"
sang Hector.

Pru sang louder
than Hector.

"I'm the star around here…"

"And once I start
I just can't stop!"
sang Hector.

"Everybody,
look at me me me!"

Pru sang so loudly she
lost her voice.

Tilly and her friends decided
to search for Pru's voice.

"I know where to find it," said Hector.
But no one was listening.

"perhaps it's under the cushions,"
said Doodle.
But it was just Tilly's button tin.

hello hello

Was Pru's voice in the tall vase?
No, it was just an echo.

"I have an idea," said Hector.

But nobody was paying attention.

"I miss pru's voice," said Tilly.

"Me too," said Tumpty.
"Even though she's a bit shouty."

"Nobody will listen to me,"
said Hector sitting on the Huff Tuffet.

Tilly and her friends
soon found him.

"Please tell us your idea, Hector,"
said Tilly.

"You'll have to come with me," said Hector,
"on the adventurous search for pru's voice."

Hector found just what
he was looking for...

Buzzz!
Buzzz!

"A JAR OF
HONEY!
It's just the thing when
you've lost your voice."

Pru took a sip
of warm honey.

Then she slurped
some more.

"My voice is back!"
she said.

"I'm ready
to sing again!"

Was it time for the Pretty Pru prance?
"Let's sing your song, Hector, because
you found my voice!" said Pru.

"There's nothing more I like to do,"
sang Hector,
"than to dance the Wiggle-Wiggle Woo."

Hooray for Tilly and her friends!

First published 2013 by Walker Books Ltd, 87 Vauxhall Walk, London SE11 5HJ

2 4 6 8 10 9 7 5 3 1

© 2012 JAM Media and Walker Productions
Based on the animated series TILLY AND FRIENDS, developed and produced by Walker Productions and JAM Media
from the Walker Books 'Tilly and Friends' by Polly Dunbar. Licensed by Walker Productions Ltd.

This book has been typeset in Gill Sans and Boopee.

Printed in China

All rights reserved. No part of this book may be reproduced, transmitted or stored in an information retrieval system
in any form or by any means, graphic, electronic or mechanical, including photocopying, taping and recording,
without prior written permission from the publisher.

British Library Cataloguing in Publication Data:
a catalogue record for this book is available from the British Library

ISBN 978-1-4063-4563-6

www.walker.co.uk

See you again soon!